Twins Take a Bath

For Simone and Anna

First Aladdin Paperbacks edition October 2003

Text copyright © 2003 by Ellen Weiss
Illustrations copyright © 2003 by Sam Williams

ALADDIN PAPERBACKS
An imprint of Simon & Schuster Children's Publishing Division
1230 Avenue of the Americas
New York, NY 10020

READY-TO-READ is a registered trademark of Simon & Schuster.

Book design by Debra Sfetsios
The text of this book was set in Century Oldstyle.

Printed in the United States of America
2 4 6 8 10 9 7 5 3 1

Library of Congress Cataloging-in-Publication Data

Weiss, Ellen.
Twins in the bath / by Ellen Weiss ; illustrated by Sam Williams.
p. cm. — (Ready-to-read)
Summary: Rhyming text describes the fun a set of twins has when they
take their bath.
ISBN 0-689-85740-3 (pbk.) — ISBN 0-689-85741-1 (lib. bdg.)
[1. Baths—Fiction. 2. Twins—Fiction. 3. Stories in rhyme.] I.
Williams, Sam, 1955– ill. II. Title. III. Series.
PZ8.3.W4245 Tx 2003
[E]—dc21
2002008969

Twins Take a Bath

By Ellen Weiss
Illustrated by Sam Williams

ALADDIN
New York London Toronto Sydney Singapore

Splash!

Splish!

I am a fish!

Yellow boat.

Watch it float.

Time for tea.

First you . . .

then me.

Fill and pour.

Have some more.

Now shampoo.

First me . . .

then you.

I have a hat.

Look at that!

The soap slides.

It slides and glides.

We are clean.

Clean as a bean.

Out of the tub.

Rub, rub, rub!

I am a lump!

You are a bump!

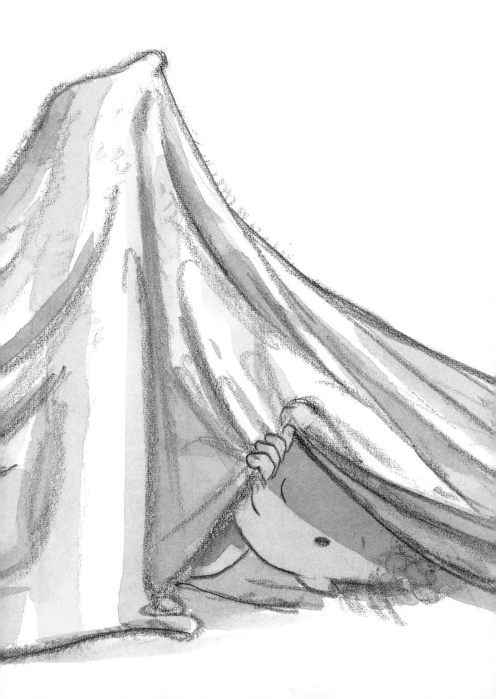

All done.
That was fun!